I0817378

HOW DO Snakes POOP?

by Malta Cunningham

Content Consultant
Charles Smith, PhD
Associate Professor of Biology
Wofford College

CAPSTONE PRESS
a capstone imprint

Bright Idea Books are published by Capstone Press
1710 Roe Crest Drive, North Mankato, Minnesota 56003
www.mycapstone.com

Library of Congress Cataloging-in-Publication Data
Names: Cunningham, Malta, 1994- author.
Title: How do snakes poop? / by Malta Cunningham.
Description: North Mankato, Minnesota : Capstone Press, [2019] | Series: Crazy animal facts | Audience: Grade 4 to 6. | Includes bibliographical references and index.
Identifiers: LCCN 2018018699 (print) | LCCN 2018022074 (ebook) | ISBN 9781543541557 (ebook) | ISBN 9781543541151 (hardcover : alk. paper)
Subjects: LCSH: Snakes--Juvenile literature. | Animal droppings--Juvenile literature.
Classification: LCC QL666.O6 (ebook) | LCC QL666.O6 C845 2019 (print) | DDC 597.96--dc23
LC record available at https://lccn.loc.gov/2018018699

Editorial Credits
Editor: Maddie Spalding
Designer: Becky Daum
Production Specialist: Laura Polzin

Photo Credits
iStockphoto: danlogan, 13, ilbusca, 31, JedsPics_com, 8–9, Mark Kostich, 16–17, MelanieMaya, 10–11; Science Source: Hugh Lansdown/FLPA/Science Source, 14–15; Shutterstock Images: beejung, 26–27, feathercollector, 21, fototrips, cover (snake), harmpeti, 18–19, 29, Heiko Kiera, 24–25, Kaliva, 22–23, Matt Jeppson, 5, phichak, cover (poop), reptiles4all, 7, Zhukov Oleg, cover (background)

Design Elements: iStockphoto, Red Line Editorial, and Shutterstock Images

TABLE OF CONTENTS

CHAPTER 1

SNAKE Surprise!

A hiker walks down a path. The sun is bright in the sky. The hiker wipes sweat off his forehead. He looks around.

He finds a rock to sit on. The rock has a dark smudge. He leans in closer. Hairs and bones are poking out. The hiker recognizes the smudge. It's snake poop!

Snakes often warm themselves on hot rocks.

CHAPTER 2

GETTING Food

A snake needs to eat before it can poop. Snakes find food in many ways. Some wait for **prey** to come to them. Others hunt for prey.

A snake uses its tongue to find prey. Prey give off chemicals. The snake's tongue picks up the chemicals. Then the snake can find the prey. The snake opens its mouth wide. It grabs its prey.

A snake flicks its tongue out of its mouth to help it find prey.

Snakes open their jaws wide to eat prey. Some can even eat deer!

Some snakes kill with **venom**. The venom comes from their **fangs**. These snakes bite their prey.

Other snakes swallow live prey. A snake's jaws are connected with tissue. The tissue is **flexible**. It allows the snake's jaws to open wide.

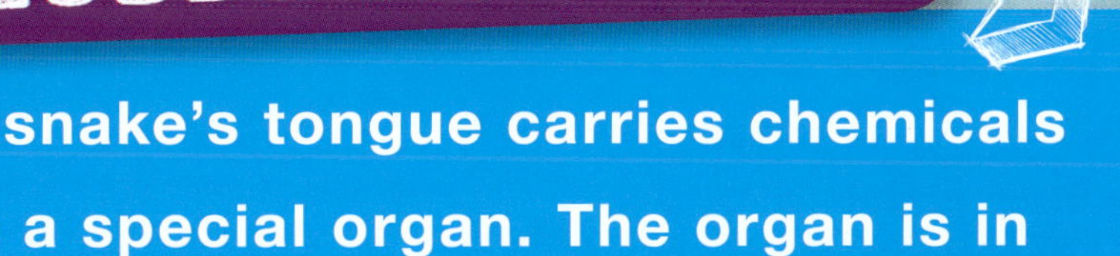

JACOBSON'S ORGAN

A snake's tongue carries chemicals to a special organ. The organ is in the roof of its mouth. This organ can identify the chemicals.

Some snakes wrap their bodies around prey. They squeeze hard. This cuts off the prey's blood supply. Its heart can't pump blood. Then the prey dies. The snake swallows it whole!

A LARGE MEAL

In Australia, a python killed and ate a crocodile. The python was 10 feet (3.1 m) long. The crocodile was 3 feet (0.9 m) long.

Squeezing prey also keeps it from escaping.

CHAPTER 3

SNAKE Poop

Prey is a snake's food. A snake needs to **digest** what it eats. Food enters the stomach. The stomach is shaped like a tube. Juices break down food. The food moves through the snake's **intestines**. It comes out as poop.

Some snakes that live in or near water eat fish.

Snake poop comes in all shapes and sizes!

Snake poop comes out of a hole. The hole is on the bottom of the snake's body. Sometimes the poop is brown. Other times it has white in it. Usually the poop is wet.

URIC ACID

A snake's digestive system breaks down proteins. This produces uric acid. This is the white part of a snake's poop.

Many snakes eat mice or rats. Bush vipers hunt prey from trees.

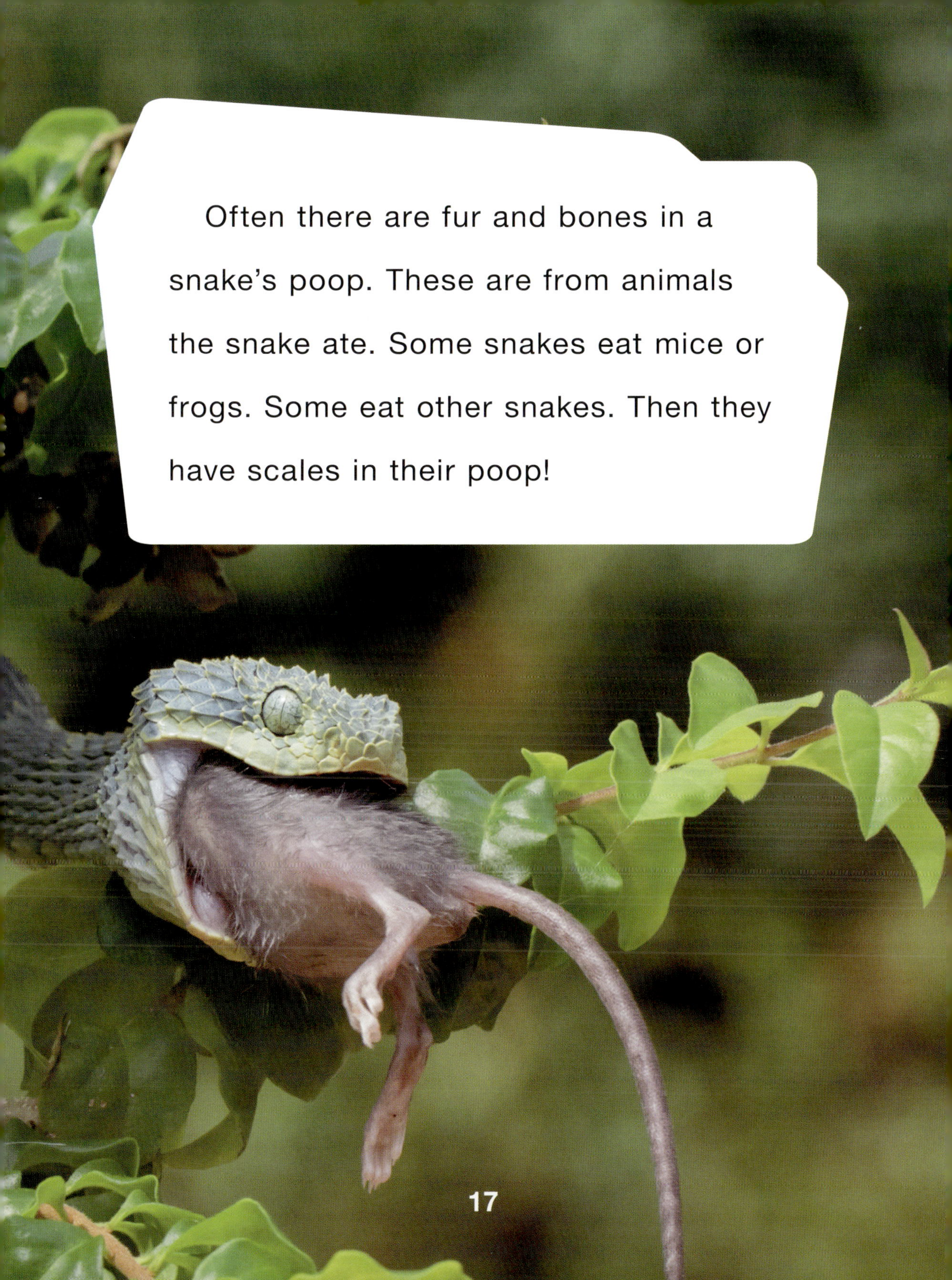

Often there are fur and bones in a snake's poop. These are from animals the snake ate. Some snakes eat mice or frogs. Some eat other snakes. Then they have scales in their poop!

HOLD IT IN!

Snakes do not eat often. They can go months without eating. This means they may not poop for months. Some pythons go more than a year without pooping. Gaboon vipers also do not poop often. This snake won't poop until it has to. One Gaboon viper went 420 days without pooping!

Gaboon vipers live in rain forests south of the Sahara Desert in Africa.

CHAPTER 4

STRANGE Snakes

Snakes usually don't eat certain toads. Some toads have poison **glands** in their skin. But one type of snake in Japan eats poisonous toads. This snake is called the tiger keelback. It can't make poison.

But it steals poison from the toads it eats. It uses the poison to protect itself. It stores the poison in glands. The glands are on the back of its neck. The snake's **predators** bite or claw its neck. This rips the skin above the glands. The predator gets a mouthful of poison!

The tiger keelback snake sneaks up on prey. It bites toads before they can hop away.

WHAT'S FOR LUNCH?

Some snakes are born with two heads. These snakes are rare. They often die in the wild. That's because both heads try to make decisions for one body. Both heads need to agree when they are hungry. They need to agree on what to eat. The two heads may fight over food. One head might try to eat the other!

Two-headed snakes may share the same stomach and digestive organs.

SNAKES THAT EAT THEIR OFFSPRING

Female snakes may give birth to many offspring. Some snakes give birth to up to 80 offspring! Their offspring are called snakelets. Some snakelets do not survive.

Most snakes lay eggs. Snakelets hatch from the eggs.

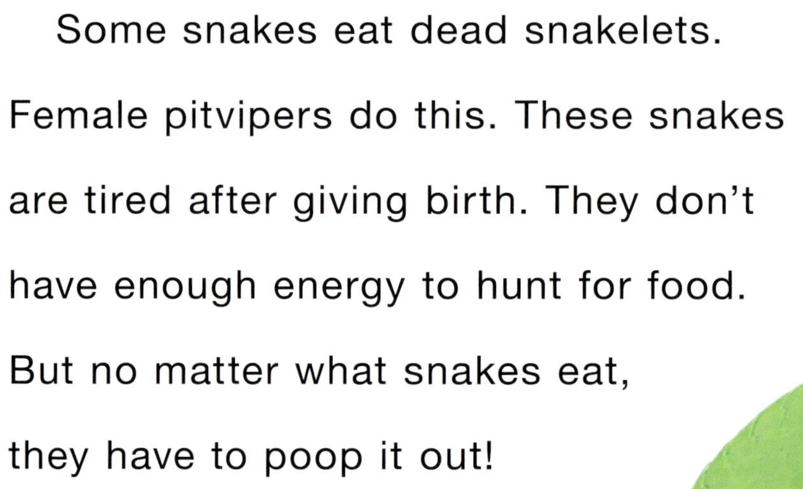

Some snakes eat dead snakelets. Female pitvipers do this. These snakes are tired after giving birth. They don't have enough energy to hunt for food. But no matter what snakes eat, they have to poop it out!

Some pitvipers live in trees.

GLOSSARY

digest
to break down food so the body can use it

fang
a long and sharp tooth that is hollow

flexible
able to move easily

gland
an organ that produces a certain substance in the body

intestine
an organ below the stomach that helps digest food

predator
an animal that kills and eats other animals

prey
an animal that is hunted by other animals for food

venom
liquid produced by some snakes that can kill prey

TOP FIVE REASONS WHY SNAKES ARE AWESOME

1. Snakes can swallow prey alive.
2. Snakes can go months without eating.
3. Some snakes may not poop for more than a year.
4. Some snakes can eat poisonous toads or newts.
5. Snakes live on every continent except Antarctica.

Snake digestion is a bit different from human digestion. To discover how, try out this simple experiment:

WHAT YOU'LL NEED

1 sealable plastic bag

2 saltine crackers

1 can or bottle of soda

INSTRUCTIONS

1. Put the crackers in the plastic bag. Seal the bag shut. Squeeze and crush the crackers.

2. Open the bag. Pour in a small amount of soda. Seal the bag. Wait a few minutes and watch what happens.

The soda has acid. Your stomach also has acid. Acid breaks down your food. Your teeth start to break down your food first. Then it enters your stomach. Crushing the crackers is similar to chewing food. But snakes do not chew their food. They swallow it whole. Snakes digest their food at a slower rate than humans do. Why do you think this is? What might food look like in a snake's stomach?

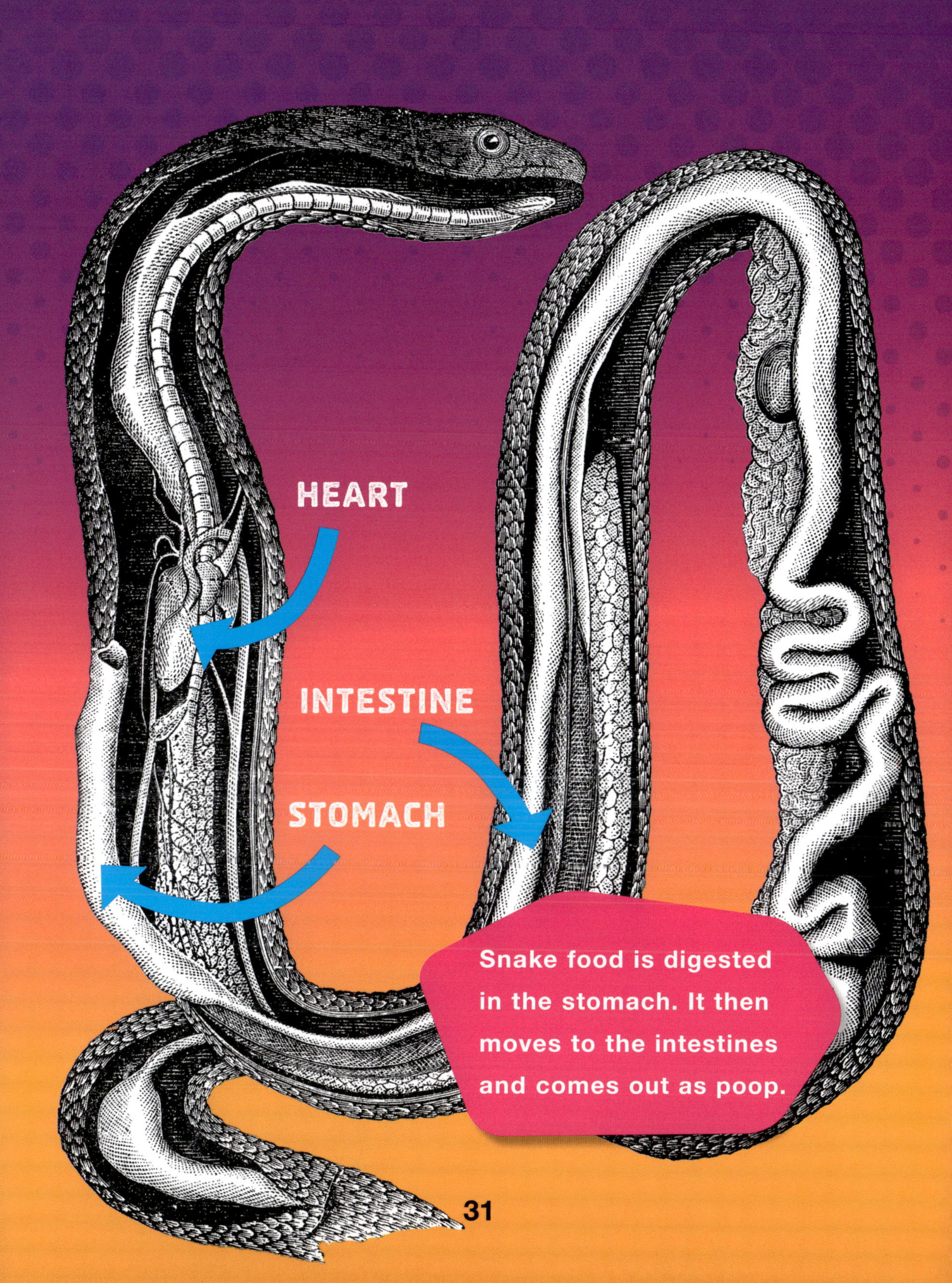

Snake food is digested in the stomach. It then moves to the intestines and comes out as poop.

FURTHER RESOURCES

Ready to discover more fun facts about snakes? Learn more with these resources:

National Geographic: Super Snakes
https://kids.nationalgeographic.com/explore/nature/super-snakes/

Stewart, Melissa. *Snakes!* Washington, D.C.: National Geographic, 2009.

Woodward, John. *Everything You Need to Know About Snakes: And Other Scaly Reptiles*. New York, NY: DK Children, 2013.

Want to learn more about different types of snakes? Check out these resources:

Alinsky, Shelby. *Slither, Snake!* Washington, D.C.: National Geographic, 2015.

National Geographic: Rattlesnake
https://kids.nationalgeographic.com/animals/rattlesnake/

INDEX